Seasons

"Seasons"

ISBN No: " 978-93-90416-13-4"
1st Edition
Language – English and Hindi

Flairs and Glairs
Publication House
Regd. Under MSME Act.

Disclaimer

This is a work of fiction and solely represent the thoughts of the corresponding authors of the articles. Our editors have tried their best to edit the content of all the authors and check the plagiarism.
All the write-ups in this book are unique and are only published in this book.
In case any plagiarism or error is found, only the author is responsible alone, and not the publisher or the Compilers.

Cover Designing and Book Formatting
Shubham Shah

Acknowledgement

Our primary thanks to our God. We are blessed with the energy to be able to complete this anthology.

We are also thankful towards our whole team of "Flairs and Glairs Publication".

Surbhi Gupta

I Offer my heartfelt gratitude to my Parents- Mr. Girish Gupta and Mrs. Neeti Gupta for always motivating and supporting me, in every aspect of my Life. Love to my friends and extended family as well, who keeps showering their Love and Blessings upon me.

Thankyou all the Co-authors , without your support we would never be able to complete this anthology.

Co-Authors

Shubham Shah (Founder Flairs and Glairs)
Ishani Agarwal (Co Founder Flairs and Glairs)
Surbhi Gupta (Compiler)

PART-1 Winter/ सर्दी का मौसम

1. Anjali Kaushal
2. Baisakhi Das
3. Deepjyoti Chowdhury
4. Dipti S
5. Hema Kirthiga J
6. Kamna Tank
7. Abhilash Sharma
8. Amruta Thakare
9. Anil Vishwakarma
10. Kuber Sharma
11. Neeti Gupta
12. Sonali Sharma Saaz

PART-2 SPRING / बसंत

13. Ananya Malhotra
14. Madhu Singh
15. Megha Anand
16. Meghna Chatterjee
17. Suhita S
18. Jasmine Panda
19. Sarabjot Purba
20. Sheikh Mohammad Junaid

PART-3 Summer / गर्मी का मौसम

21. Ashima Jain
22. Prachi Gupta
23. Shresth Bhargava (Yash)

24. Shubham Mohite
25. Surekha Wankhede
26. Tanupreet Kaur
27. Arun Kashyap

PART-4 Monsoon / मानसून

28. Akanksha Sakhuja
29. Archana Devi
30. Dr. Ratna Priyanka Bhallamudi
31. E. Sindhuvarshini
32. Isha Saraiya
33. Nivedhitha Patwari
34. Samikhya Swain
35. Shijin Ravi C
36. Sujitha Ramalingam
37. Akanksha Sinha
38. Harsha Sharma
39. Neha Singhania
40. Padma Srivastava
41. Sahina Ghugha
42. Sarbani Dey
43. Shivika Sharma
44. Urvashi Patel

PART-5 Fall/Autumn / पतझड़

45. Aditi Debnath
46. Jude Fernandes
47. Prittam Bhattacharyya
48. Rashi Sunder
49. Soma Das
50. Ujjwal Shree

Shubham Shah

(Founder- Flairs and Glairs)

Shubham Shah, entrepreneur at “Flairs & Glairs” a brand with dynamics in events organizing and cultural educational pan INDIA, He is a 26yr. old guy who recently has entered, the digital platform of imprinting emotions. He has initiated with his own open mic platform to help budding poets and aspiring writers under his brand named as “Teekhe Zasbaaat” He is a commerce graduate from Bhagalpur City of Bihar.

He says Writing has impersonated him since childhood and he has now been writing for over a decade!

Cooking, on the other hand, is his passion! He also mentions, trying out new things just tickles him!

When asked sir, Why SPICY EMOTIONS?

He smiled and added, “agar jasbaat teekhe na ho toh wo jasbaat kaha” Spices are all that blends! So do his words!
As a chef, he presents to you his dish! Hot and freshly served! Taste it! Feel it! Enjoy it! You can also find his writing in the Solo book “Teekhe Zasbaaat” and 70+ anthologies. With his passion to explore opportunities across Platforms he is working with keen devotion and We wish him all the very best for his future ventures
Share your reviews on his

INSTAGRAM

@spicy_emotions
@shubham4shah

Or via email on

shubham2shah@gmail.com

To stay tuned to his work and opportunities follow his business Handles

INSTAGRAM FACEBOOK YOUTUBE

@flairsandglairs
@teekhezasbaaat

WEBSITE:

https://flairsandglairs.in/
https://flairsandglairs.com/

Ishani Agarwal

(Co Founder- Flairs and Glairs)

Ishani Agarwal

Born and brought up in Kolkata, she has done her schooling and college from here itself. She is doing her post-graduation at the moment. Ishani loves talking to people around, and is excited for this new beginning of hers! Been a Compiler for 35+ Anthologies, and in the process for more, also, co-authored in 100+ Anthologies, Ishani is very Happy with how her life is turning out now!

Insta handle: Ishani_agarwal_quotes

Surbhi Gupta (Compiler)

Surbhi Gupta, born and raised in Punjab, is currently a Law Student , B.Com honours graduate and an enthusiastic writer as well. She is also working as Project Head for Flairs And Glairs Publications. Having a Lawyer's mind and a writer's heart, her writings are sui generis, relatable, and inspiring. She is part of various writing events , communities and anthologies as both compiler and co-author. Various achievements in academics , Legal events and writing platforms are feathers in her cap. Sight and smell of her own book someday is what she aspires to achieve as a writer.

Instagram Handle- @surbhi_writes
Email Id- surbhigupta855@gmail.com

The Multicolor Mellow
(Autumn)

A Pleasant, blissful and multicolor mellow
that appeases one's heart, especially mine
Just the balance I desire,
a cool-off from scorching heat or chilly cold
Autumn brings us the sunshine,
blended with a cool breeze in galore
Orange, red, amber and yellow hues in the leaves,
Yes! this is the season of maturity
Nature is at its best with its scenic beauty
A feast to the eyes ,
a lesson of hope for the life,
the calming effect drawn by equinox
provides a break from the hectic working hours
It is fall, my beloved season
Full of festivities, and some magical fantasies
starting the trend of those cozy apparels
long boots and warm woolen mittens
spicy lattes and mochas with syrups,
"Happy Holidays" becomes the famous phrase
Simply merrymaking family days
Autumn has a lot deeper meaning,
to the ones who choose to look within,
We meet every year,
yes, I am in love with this season...forever

PART-1

Winter/

Anjali Kaushal

Anjali is a budding writer and she loves reading fictional stories.
Instagram Handle @anjalikaushal

The White Season

In many places winter has been used to symbolize harshness, silence, loneliness and death. People don't like this season. But if one sees carefully, it has many perks. In winters there is freshness in the air. In many parts of the world Christmas falls during winter and its magic is spread all around. It's the season of lights. The children can be seen making snowmans and playing in the snow. It's just impossible to imagine Christmas without snow. When snowfall occurs snowflakes that fall from the sky bring another magical experience. The shape of each and every snowflake is different which puts people in astonishment. Seeing the scientific side, the metabolism of many bacterias stop working in cold weather and therefore there are fewer diseases. Travelling in winters is easier. The sun rays in winters bring comforting warmth with it, unlike that of summers that makes us sweat. It's the blooming season in India. Winter does mark the end of a year but every ending is a new beginning. All people need to do is to find beauty in this season just like Robert Frost did in his poem "Stopping by the woods on a snowy evening" where he gets enchanted on seeing the trees getting covered with snow. Every season is beautiful and has positivity in them then why only see the negative traits. Writers should explore the beautiful side of winter and change the usual symbolism of winter.

Baisakhi Das

Baisakhi Das, a young girl from the city of joy, Kolkata which is situated in West Bengal. She has an amazing passion for writing and has written over 50 contents on Pratilipi, an online social media site based on stories, poems, novels, etc. Her stories and poems are read by over 6.5 thousand peoples and she is the co author of 70 anthologies. Instagram handle @baisakhi.das.5686

Winter

Winter! Well what more is there to say
For winter can only be described in one way
With just one word I think everyone will know
That beautiful crystal like crunchy stuff that is snow
Every year I pray at night
That in the morning I'll see a blanket of white
Then I'll find out that school is shut
So I run outside and into the snow my feet cut
They make deep marks in the snow delicate skin
But then we will snowball fight and I know I'll win
Then we will make a snow lady and call her Gladyss
But the next morning I will miss
The snow lady's rounded figure
But what's this? I snowed again now everything's bigger!
But when it starts to get really cold,
I will go inside for a cup of hot cocoa
Though the snow is thick and it will be here for long
I know I will wake up one morning and Gladyss with be gone

Deepjyoti Chowdhury

Deepjyoti Chowdhury embraces reading and writing as her escape from the real world as well as a window to it. She is a strong believer of Christ and Karma. Currently pursuing Master's in English literature, she has written in 100+ anthologies, she is the author of "Heartfelt musings" and "The staircase to freedom". Her main aim is to heal people and make them smile through her art of writing.

Instagram Handle @dj_writes_to_heal .

The Seasonal Bliss

Sometimes I feel winter is the best,
When under a comfy quilt unendlessly we rest.
Hot stuffs to eat and drink we request,
With multiple comfy dresses we're dressed.

Then I feel summer is a bliss,
As we can eat all cold dishes.
Ice creams and cold drink brings no sickness,
New fruits and vegies we gladly witness.

Autumn and Spring are no less,
But out of all Winter I find the best.
As unending comfort and sleep it rewards,
Comes like a friend and leaves like a guest.

Dipti. S

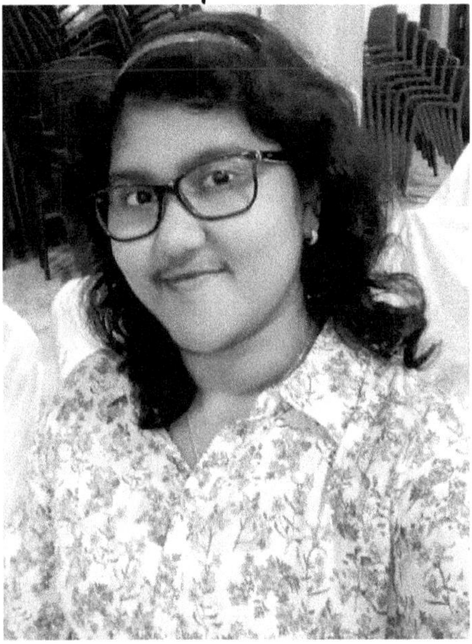

Dipti. S is an aspiring author who aims to become a published author soon. She is currently exploring in all types of writing. She is preparing to clear NET exam to become a professor. She is an avid reader and loves listening to music. She completed her Bachelors degree in English at Lady Doak College and her Masters degree in English at The American College. She currently resides in Madurai.
Instagram Handle @dipti_david

The Time Of Amazing Cold

Yes, the time of winter is an amazing season of the year where joy fills the earth and the atmosphere is very cheerful as the season's greetings flood the cities. It is the time of the year where the chilly whether brings us season's cheers! Christmas adds a sparkle to the wintery whether as the season of cold and snow comes forth gushing in it's own splendour. As the smell of new delicious treats and the charming aroma of chocolates, cakes, and bakes fill the air. And the desire to shop doesn't seem to quench and you continue to be a shopaholic. This is the time of December which appears to be blasphemous of them all where you feel like getting away with almost anything and have a fresh start from the new year's eve by disciplining yourself through new year's resolutions. Of course the December month is the month of Christmas and New year which fills us with immeasurable glee, and tidings of comfort and joy. And the season's cheers overflow. And, this is also a season where you could see a warm smile on the face of the needy. And the warmth of that smile lights up a fire on the inside of our hearts which warms us up and lights up our soul. And, yes this is the month of the December cold. This is the season, the season of amazing cold.

Hema Kirthiga J

She is Hema Kirthiga J, and her pen name is sparkle. She is professionally a psychologist and passionately a writer. She heals others but writing heals her. She is writer, reader, orator and a believer. She is from Chennai. She lives by the principal of inspire and be inspired. She writes her heart and soul and she deeply believes that the depth of her heart and the nib of her pen are soulfully connected. Writing is an art and she is a proud artist. She loves what she does and loves what she writes. You can reach her at

Instagram Handle @the_pen_queen
Email- inker.sparkle@gmail.com
Yourquote – JKM

The Golden Days

The snow outside the house!
You by my side!
Love in the heart!
Joy in the room!
Life was awesome!!!!
A hot cup of tea!
And a lot of cuddle!
With a melody music,
Or a favorite movie!
With the hot evening snack!
And no one to disturb!
With the love in the air!
Dreams on the roll!
Deep in the bed sheet!
Rolled by you!!!

Was the perfect winter days!!
The season I love...

Kamna Tank

Kamna Tank is a Dietician By Profession and Writer by passion. She loves to Portrays Emotions on paper to encourage herself about feelings Apart from writing Drawing, Travelling, Listening Music Is her passion She always love to create something new. She Always Ready To Tackle With New World
Instagram Handle @kittykitts2

Winter Blossoming

Season has its own aroma to attract
Winter is one of the best in the bucket list of wonderland
That cold breeze in early morning
That frozen hand under the blanket
All the foggy weather outside try to hide the site
Those beautiful sleepy moments which is actually the best time
That icy lakes and ponds shines like a rare diamond that no one can deny
Cloud runs fast and looks like hiding us
Hills get covered in a beautiful white layer of ice
Which attract a travelers and the photographers
To take picture of nature's beautiful season
Its winter that oozes the body
And create a shivering moment that is actually a Magical.

Abhilash Sharma

Abhilash Sharma a 23 year old passionate writer. He belongs to Sonipat , Haryana . He had completed his B.com (voc) recently. He is a enthusiastic person and a sports lover as well .Worked as a co author in about 40+ anthologies inspired by Ishika Arora and Ishani Aggarwal in the field of writing .You can check out his writings on
Instagram Handle @_ankahe_alfaaz_

वो प्यारी सी सर्दी

वो प्यारी सी सर्दी ,
ना देती गर्मी जैसे बेदर्दी ,

ओस की वो चादर लाती ,
सबको कंबलों में छुपाती ,

अक्सर सभी को लुभाती ,
कभी कभी ये डराती ,

तेज़ हवाओं से ये मिलाती ,
दांतों तले जीभ दबवाती ,

सूरज के दर्शन को तरसाती ,
कभी कभी खूब तड़पाती ,

अपने पैरों पर नचाती ,
तो कभी गलियों गलियों
में घुमाती ।।

Amruta Thakare

Amruta Thakare is Passionate Writer. She is from Maharashtra. Amruta is an undergraduate student from Nashik University. She love to speak truth and write by heart in the form of Poems, Shayari, One liners, Microtale. Her hobbies apart from Writing includes Dancing, Singing, Anchoring, Reading books as well.

Instagram Handle @_nayisoch

सर्दियों की झलक मेरे दिल में समाई

सर्दियों का मौसम कुछ ऐसें आया
कोहरे से नया सवेरा जगमगया,
मानो जैसे नई जिंदगी मिली हो,
पसंदीदा ये मौसम मैंने हैं पाया।

इंतज़ार हर घड़ी इस मौसम का मुझे,
हर दिनों को अपने ख्यालों में सजाया,
वह कांपकपाते दातों की टिक टिक,तो
थंड भरी हवाओं ने मुझे हैं उलझाया,
मासुमियत छुपी इन महीनों में, दिल से
पसंदीदा मौसम मैंने सर्दियों का पाया।

सिगडी की सेक तो वह गर्महाट लिए,
साथ में चाय की मज़ा कुछ अलग सी आई,
खुबसूर्ति थंड भरी नजारों में,
गरमागरम मुंगफल्लि की सुगंध फ़ैलाई,
हर बदलते मौसमो से समाधान पर, सबसे
पसंदीदा मौसम मैंने सर्दियाँ ही पाई।

ठंड की वर्दी सबने हैं पहनी, तो
सुकड़ सी सबकी चाल हो गई,
कोई गर्महाट की कंभल ओढ़े सोया तो,
नाक सबकी लाल हो गई,
कोहरे भरी रातों में सुकून की निंद,
तो चहेरे पर अलग सी चमक लहराई,
इंतज़ार रहा मुझे इन दिनों का, क्योंकि
सर्दियों की झलक मेरे दिल में समाई।।

Anil Vishwakarma

The Co-author is known as Shri Anil Kumar Vishwakarma, he belongs to the capital of the country, Delhi. He received his undergraduate education from Delhi University and is currently working in a prestigious organization. He is a serious and responsible youth as well as a dutiful and family man. He keeps his writing interest alive even when he is busy with the daily tasks of his life. It was during his post-graduation that interest in writing arose in him, but it took him some time to materialize this art. The inspiration and source of his writing is his beloved life partner. He is a bit taciturn, but through a pen he knows how to speak. He wants to connect with you through their writings and poems and at the same time wish that you also encourage and give affection to him because he is still new in this field but wants to go further in this journey.
Instagram Handle @anil0287

सर्द रातें

वो पौष माह की जाड़े की रात, क्या हसीन रात होती है,
अंगीठी के सामने बैठ कर, सबसे ढ़ेर सारी बात होती है।

रजाई में घुस, कर पाते हैं बातें, बाहर थोड़ी बरसात होती है,
सारा साल जो करते है इंतज़ार, उनकी फिर बारात होती है।

नींद गहरी आती है बहुत, तकिया भी अपने साथ सोती है,
उठने का नहीं करता है मन, जब भी कोई आहट होती है।

प्यार जब हद से ज्यादा बढ़ जाए, दिल में घबराहट होती है,
सर्दरात में कोई लिपट के सो जाये, ऐसी बस चाहत होती है।

मज़ा नहीं कोई गर्मी और बरसात में, ये सर्दी ख़ास होती है,
इसी मौसम में ही तो सबके प्यार की नई शुरुआत होती है।

ठंड

ये ठंड भी बड़ी बेरहम है, कुवारों के लिये,
महबूब की याद दिलाती है,
वो लोग खुशनसीब होते है,
जिनकी ठंड में शादी हो जाती है।

Kuber Sharma

He is an energetic Man. Full of Passion. Writing Poetry is his only passion. He wrote Poetries near about 700. And his work is still going on. Completed his graduation .
Instagram Handle @Kuber.58

ठंड का प्रकोप

उदासी सी छाई रहती है दिन भर,
रजाई में बैठे रहने का मन करता है,
ठंडी हवा जो चलती है आसमान में,
परिंदा भी उड़ने से डरता है,
घर में रहने वाला तो रजाई में बैठ जाता है,
पर बिना घर का इंसान तो बेचारा ठंड में ही मरता है,

आसान नही ठंड में जीना,
ज़िन्दगी मानो बन्द पड़ जाती है,
अक्टूबर - नवंबर तक तो ठीक होता है मौसम,
पर असली ठंड तो दिसंबर - जनवरी में सताती है ।

Neeti Gupta

Neeti Gupta, born and raised in Punjab, is a Homemaker and an enthusiastic writer as well She is part of various writing communities, events and anthologies. Her writings are inspired by mythology, Philosphy and real life situations. Her hobbies, apart from writing includes cooking, drawing and singing as well. Her family is most dearest to her.

मौसम सर्दी का

सबसे प्यारा सर्दी का
ठिठूरती ठण्ड कड़कती धूप का
गचचक रेवड़ी और मूंगफली का
छुटकारा पसीने वाली गर्मी का
सुन्दर स्वेटर और जैकटों का
अंधेरे कमरे में हीटर जलाने का
लोहड़ी में रंग बिरंगी पतंगों का
साग मक्खन मक्की की रोटी का
सर्दी का मौसम है सबसे अच्छा
न छिपकली, मच्छर न तिलचट्टा
लगे नयारा मौसम सर्दी का
मौसम न कोई इस जैसा
मिलकर धूप में बैठना
जहाँ जहाँ धूप खिसकते जाना
काम कर लें चाहे जितना
न लगे गर्मी न आए पसीना
सबको भाए ये सर्दी का मौसम
जोश जगाए सभी में ये मौसम

Sonali Sharma "Saaz"

She is Sonali Sharma "Saaz" from indore, MP. Sonali has done her graduation from Amity university, and now she is pursuing Masters in Psychology. She has started writing from 9th standard and that was her hobby but now it becomes her passion. basically, she writes stories, quotes, microtales, shayris, poems and now she is building her way towards her dreams. She has worked as a Co author in many books and she is a compiler too.
Instagram Handle @hear_my_heart_silently

इंतज़ार

मेरी मोहब्बत में मौसम हज़ार हैं,
तुम्हारे आने का बस इंतज़ार है।

जाड़े की चारो पहर सी हो तुम,
कभी कोहरे की कहर सी हो तुम,
कभी दिन की मीठी धूप, कभी ओस भी हो तुम,

फीकी हैं सारी वादियाँ, तुम्हारे आगे सब बेकार है,
तुम्हारे आने का बस इंतज़ार है।।

यूँ जाती सर्दियाँ भी अब तुम्हें बुलाया करती हैं,
तुम आओगी, बहार के गीत गाया करती हैं,
ज़िस्म छोड़ो! तुम्हारे अक्स से भी हमें प्यार है,

एक मात्र तुम्हारे साथ होने की बस दरकार है,
तुम्हारे आने का बस इंतज़ार है।।

मेरी जाड़े सी मोहब्बत

मेरी शॉल बनकर मुझसे लिपटे रहो,
मुझे डर है कि कहीं बर्फ़ ना हो जाऊँ मैं।।

तुम कोहरे सी मुझे हर तरफ़ से घेरे रहो,
सर्द हवा बन, तुझमें ही रम जाऊँ मैं।।

जो दिन को मीठी धूप बादलों से झाँके,
तेरा सिरहाना ले, तेरी गोद में सो जाऊँ मैं।।

यूँ अलविदा लेता सूरज भी कल आएगा,
तू भी आने का वादा कर, सिर्फ़ तेरे लिए शाम हो जाऊँ मैं..

यूँ तो अक्सर जाड़ा ख़ूब नाजुक बना देता है,
बस अब चाहत है कि बहक कर सम्भल भी जाऊँ मैं।।

PART-2

Spring / बसंत

Ananya Malhotra

Ananya is a 16-year old teen, hailing from Punjab, who started writing when she was 11. Winning awards and recognitions for her work, set the true fire in her to take up poetry writing as her hobby. She is a student of grade 11 who writes to inspire people around her, through the fragrance of her compositions. She believes in being good, and doing good to all.

Instagram Handle @ananya_thepoetic

Spring Is Bliss

Rebirth, renewal, and euphoria is all around,
Coz' spring has enveloped the air and the ground..
Spring is bliss! Spring is bliss!
The only season that I dearly miss..

Lush green landscapes and feathery trees,
Temperature neither hot nor one to freeze!
Bask in the sun or lie out in your lawn,
Spring will rejuvenate you till night from morn' .
Spring is bliss! Spring is bliss!
So many bounties, without being amiss

The breeze tosses my hair over my face,
Enlightens me, and brings the long-awaited glace
Perhaps it was forlorn in the other comrades of spring,
Look, how eternally, bliss does it bring!!
O, beautiful, heavenly spring!!

Madhu Singh

Her name is Madhu Singh .she love to write motivational, inspirational, and emotional quotes .She started writing in March 2020 and very soon she became a part of flairs and glairs as a co-author in the face of flairs and glairs she get a bit success in lit age .She is hard-working and determined girl who never give up in any situation and she also make others motivate .she is a simple girl who love to talk and help and care about others .Most of the people called her an innocent girl .She love to enjoy and captured each and every moment of her life

Instagram Handle @ Madhusingh4236

Spring

Spring is the season of pleasant.
Spring is the bloom .
Spring is the season of love and everyone loves this season, because they have fun .
Spring is the season of flower and flower heal the heart of our .
Spring is the season of sunshine which bright up in our life .
This season make us feel blessed at every time .
That's why i feel every time alive.
I love to bloom like flower in the spring season time .
Make you also feel alive have happy spring season to my life.

Megha Anand

"A dreamer from Delhi , studies in Delhi University. Writing gives her immense pleasure . She tries to mold her thoughts into words. "
Instagram Handle @anandmehu

Spring Blossom

The way this universe look at you, do you look at it the same way. The way spring spreads love in the atmosphere ,do you spread love the same way

Spring brings happiness joy and motivation ,it helps us to see the beauty of nature, that even if it becomes dark at night, there's a beautiful morning ,beautiful start everyday

Spring brings the message that giving Is not always a loss as it gives us beautiful view, flowers, grass, trees, sound, breeze.

Yes it has its own way of taking it all back during autumn .

The mobility birds show in the spring is the lesson that everything from the nature is equally distributed everywhere, there's no discrimination. We discriminate love for our every relationship instead.

Knowing this, we ruin the beauty of nature instead of Beautify it. We feel joy in plucking flowers and keeping them. We think storing them is alluring, fascinating and graceful.

Unknowingly we are hurting ourselves . This is maybe the revenge that nature places during autumn . It snatches all of the graceful, and fascinating flowers, insects, birds, breeze and give us snivel, whining, sad surroundings.

Giving limitless is a loss. Giving it in a limit can give us opportunities, it's a boon.

Understanding the lesson the nature teaches us is the wisest thing you can ever do.

Meghna Chatterjee

She is a simple girl with the simplest dream of spreading smiles and cheers all around.
Instagram Handle @ Meghna Chatterjee

The Colourful Spell

Oh dear spring you unravel in bounty the ecstatic fervour of luminescence and splendor,
With the brilliant strokes your magical marvel you behold a majestic wonder
Your addictive ,mellow sunshine and your wind blowing mild
Makes the freezing spirits of exhubarance rise again and turns grappling winter the quitude blazing and wild.
Your splendid reds , the vibrant oranges , the jubilant yellows and the dazzling pinks
Writes in the despairing heart ,new stories of hope in glittering inks.
The naive little buds of your beautiful flowers and the soothing chords of your lush green ripples
They all give a message of rejuvination and reminiscence when a colourless despair unfolds and a gloom of sadness grapples.
The enthralling enemour of the cheerful melody of your birds merry and soulful.
You unfold a Dreamland of reality astonishingly addictive and beautiful.

Suhita S

Suhita, admitted for MA in English Literature, a Charming girl, who loves the magical spark of life on holding the air of positivism, her love for crazy fantasies never ends, she acts to make the most of every second by loving the simplest form of each individuals. She had been Co-author of 18+ anthologies under various publications and many more in progress. She is also a book reviewer. Her poems are published in the Magazine 'Artistic Athena' of June and July edition and in Digital Magazine 'Shelves Of Arts and Literature' Volume-1. She observes and feels everything by heart, spreading her colours all over. Her thoughts were soulfully penned!

Instagram Handle @sparkling_wink
Mail Id: suhichutty171@gmail.com

Spring Days

Season of spring spinned as my favourite
Were the hope of bud blooms
Restoring the lost confidence
With the achieved experience
After please and heal throughout,
Paving way for new jaunt
Colourful destiny in the fullness of time!

But at the present moment
I undergo pleasure and pain
Since I realize this day as an end
Of my undergraduate,
Sense of happiness peaks by successful fulfillment
With unexplainable emptiness on my heart!
The missing touch is holded and stopped without expressing,

A family began with simple smile
And ended abruptly without a proper bye
I am in search of self in the ocean of emotion
Craving to meet my crew at least for a time again!

Jasmine Panda

Jasmine Panda is presently pursuing M.Sc. Chemistry from Berhampur University, Bhanjanagar, Odisha, India. She is a Gold Medalist and University Topper in her B.Sc. She is also continuing an internship CSIR-SRTP in IICT Hyderabad. She is a Governor Awardee for Youth Red Cross. She has received All-Rounder Award in her 12th standard. She has been Literary and Cultural Champion in her college days. She has also cracked a campus in Vedanta. She has been appreciated as an anchor in many International events. She has completed Masters in Fine Arts (MFA) from Bangeeya Sangeet Parishad and done a computer course PGDCA. She is an amiable person interested in both Science and Literature. Publishing her own book someday is something which she aspires!

आगमन ऋतुराज का

देखो ऋतुराज आया है, शोभा का भंडार लाया है!!

ऋतुओं का राजा ऋतुराज आया है,
सौंदर्य का चादर साथ लाया है!
नवपल्लबों नवकुसुमों चारों ओर है,
प्राकृतिक सुंदरता अब मनोरम है!!

हरियाली में लहराते सरसों के फूल,
दुल्हन रूपी प्रकृति आज है मसगुल!
देखो, हरे हरे घाघरे, पीली सी चुनर,
अपनी शोभा बिखेर, करती है श्रृंगार!!

मधुर मधुर सा प्रकृति का संगीत,
अब तन मन करता है आनंदित!
मस्त हवाओं के झोकें से विमोहित,
वाह! प्रकृति रानी आज है सुसज्जित!!

बोल रही है कोयल टहनियों पर,
देखो, पुलकित होकर नाचती है मोर!
धीरे धीरे लग रहे हैं बोरे अब पेड़ों पर,
वाह! ऋतुराज! आश्चर्यचकित है अंबर!!

आया है वसंत पंचमी का त्योहार,
नई उमंग लाया मौसम का बाहर!
मंत्र मुग्ध करता पक्षियों का कलरव,
तितलियां और भ्रमरें मंडराते है जब!!

कुछ शरमाई सी है प्रकृति रानी,
लाई है त्योहार रंग बिरंगी होली!

जमा है राधा कृष्ण रास का रंग,
लीला रचते हैं गोपियों के संग!!

सुंदर मोहक दृश्य करता है अमोदित,
नई रूप में प्रकृति आज सुशोभित!
प्रकृति और ऋतुराज का यह संगम,
जैसे मिला हो धरती को नया जीवन!!

देखो ऋतुराज आया है, शोभा का भंडार लाया है!!

Sarabjot Purba

Sarabjot Purba lives in Kotkapura, Punjab. He wrote a poem for the first time when he was in class XI. After this While studying E.T.T., he started writing poems as well as essays and stories. He has given the thoughts of his mind in the form of a book. Whose name is 'Kuz Vichar'. He also wrote some pages related to E.T.T. College time. He has written something on every subject. He often writes on issues of society. He mostly use Punjabi language.
Instagram Handle @purba_poetry

बसंत

बसंत सूहावनी आई है,
साथ में खुशीया लेकर आई है।
है यह सबसे सुंदर मौसम,
यह बात प्राकृति ने बताई है,
कोई शक नहीं है इसमें,
पक्षीयो ने चहचहाहट सुनाई है।
सुंदर फूल है चारो ओर,
यहाँ देखो हरियाली छाई है।
रंग-बिरंगे फूलों ने तो,
आत्मा रंग-बिरंगी बनाई है।
मन को कितना सूकून है देती,
आवाज़ कोयल ने जो सुनाई है।
नदी का पानी शुद्ध है अब,
जिस से हमने प्यास बुझाई है।
आँखें कैसे भूल सकती है,
मुस्कुराहट हर चेहरे पर जो लाई है।

Sheikh Mohammad Junaid

He is "SHEIKH MOHAMMAD JUNAID" from Bhopal Madhya Pradesh. He is a student of b.ed and he is also an accountant. He has been active in the field of writing for the last 3 years. He have been active on "YOUR QUOTE" since may 2020 and have written many ghazals on it. Mostly he write on love but sometimes his thoughts are also focused on other subjects. When his mood is at a different level, it often creates poetry. He have the ability to put his emotions into words.

Whenever he writes something, he is dedicated to someone.

Email - mohammadjunaid078603@gmail.com

बहार (ग़ज़ल)

बहार आई और दिल गुलज़ार हो गए,
हम अपने ही गमो के गमख़्वार हो गए,

दरीचे बंद नहीं हुए हमारे दिल के और,
दिमाग से अपने हम यूं पुरबहार हो गए,

बहार की चमक क्या फैली चारों तरफ,
हमारे तो हर इक दिन ख़ुशगवार हो गए,

जो आया है अब मौसम-ए-बहार का तो,
ख़िज़ाँ के रंग भी तो रंग-ए-बहार हो गए,

बाद-ए-बहार गुलिस्ताँ सारे महका गई,
गुल भी खिलकर अब ज़रनिगार हो गए,

मौसम-ए-बहार तो प्यार का मौसम है,
अफ़सुर्दा वजूद वाले भी दिलदार हो गए,

जश्न-ए-बहार जुनैद कितने दिलकश थे,
गुज़री बहार तो सारे पल यादगार हो गए ।

PART-3

Summer /

गर्मी का मौसम

Ashima Jain

She is passionate about her work. She is honest and loves to accepting the new challenges. She is loyal. She knows cooking dancing etc. She is openhearted and open minded.
Instagram Handle @ashima3766

Summer days

The sun, it fades in the moonlight.
The stars, they fade in the daylight.

The cold breezes are strong in winter and spring,
And the warm, sunny days are what summer brings.

The ice cream van's song plays a tune as the children play on the sand,
The joy on their little faces as their parents put money in their small, little hands.

I remember the time when my dad put me on his shoulders as we surfed in the waves,
And all the times he would put on a song and we would have our own little rave.

I remember the time when I made sand castles with my friends and the joy we all had.
I remember the summer days, and not a memory of those bright, sunny days was bad.

Prachi Gupta

Prachi Gupta is a student of BBA, hailing from Allahabad, UP. She is fond of watching movies, cooking and singing. She loves to travel, reading books and writing. She has also been a co-author of many anthologies and participated in many online competition in which she has won some of the achievement for her best write-ups.
Instagram Handle @_prachi_gupta_210

Summer

Mostly, I don't like this season
But I just feel more comfortable in this than rest.

Mostly, it's a bit exuding
But, it feels good if you have a fan with you.

Mostly, it is a hottest and sunset occurs at its highest
But, it's fine if you have a cucumber and lime.

I think it's a good season for a reason,
For getting holidays
For a day lengths.
For spending time with loved ones..

Mostly, it's season of rest, peace and shine
People can easily go for ride and do swim

It's a great endeavour to complete your task in a little time span
Without shivering, soaking and worrying.

I just love the season of summer
It stays forever in my heart and mind.

Shresth Bhargava (Yash)

Shresth Bhargava (Yash), is an emerging writer,author as well as compiler from The city of Love, The city of Taj AGRA.In his point of view , 'we can bring positive changes in the lives of peoples as well as we can ir-radicate social-evil's from our community by the help of our writings'.Apart from his writtings ,he is also a CA Aspirant ,His aim of life is to help mankind and bring positive changes in the lives of his countrymen .He has won various certificates in various competitions,He is always there for help of peoples in need .He is nature loving person,He is a devotee of Lord Shiva .He respect the ones who respects him and himself .He is verey friendly person,for him his family and friends is his lifeline
Intagram ID @yashbhargava2000

Summer

Oh sun god why bother
Why would it be so hot that everyone's life was lost,
Why don't we pity
We die in heat every second
The streets would be deserted
When you climb the summit,
How do we get relief
Give me some knowledge
Oh sun god why bother
Why would everyone get so hot that everyone's life turned out?
Those who would get wet at the moment of power loss
Then no one would lose work
Ever change the weather by mistake
After getting the rain water all the bails would have been melted,
But when showing your appearance
The whole world is confused
Oh sun god why bother
Why would everyone get so hot that everyone's life turned out?

Shubham Mohite

Amateur writer with considerate passion for -'Poetic Shorts' .
Instagram Handle @small_mindful_notes

Why Does It Hurt?

On a shiny day,
Being in my shorts,
I stood on the beach,
With my feet sunk deep.

Yes! right into the grainy sand,
With waves hitting me forth and back
Causing tickles beneath it,
Making me happy! As I could feel it.

Cool breeze was flowing in,
And the sea was all calm,
I was lost into thinking,
About the view I was reminiscing...

The days of peace were gone,
As I sit behind the working desk,
With flickering screens and unrest!
Where nothing seemed to be of interest.

The summertime of a teenager,
It was lost & forgone,
Becoming a responsible adult,
I ask - "Why does it hurt?"
Just tell me please,
That why does it hurt!

Surekha Wankhede

Surekha Wankhede, a very passionate girl. She belongs to city of Oranges, Nagpur, Maharashtra. Apart than writing she loves to do Classical dance. She has worked as co-author in many anthologies including World Records too. An optimistic and keen observant girl.
Instagram Handle @nuance_sayings

My favourite season of the year is Summer. It is the season of love.

The warm weather, the school vacations, and the endless fun is just mesmerizing. As well as it is the perfect atmosphere to do outdoor activities. Summer is the only one season when you are free to do whatever you want, not worrying about homework, studies or waking up early for school. Summer is like something to spend your weekends with you loving cousins, easy road trips with full of fun and joy.

Tanupreet Kaur

Tanupreet Kaur is born and brought up in New Delhi, India and a graduate in bachelor of arts along with the certification in Creative Writing, German Language and Desktop Publishing. She has been writing since 2016 to achieve the expression of her life and finding solace. She started this journey with writing quotes firstly then poetry and finally short stories and to know her more you can check her Instagram handle : @_heavenofdiversions_

Oh My Dear Summers

If someone asks me about my favourite season,
without a second thought,
I would say summer.

At times monsoon and winter are overrated,
eventually underrating the summer,
almost every other day.

But it isn't my favourite,
not only just my birthday month lies in,
but also cause' of the memories it holds.

School summer vacations,
Home coming of mangoes,
my never ending love for them.

Crying over holiday homework,
Playing most of the time with friends,
my never ending love for them.

Chilles of heat,
first sip of ice candies,
my never ending love for them.

Constant irritation of sweat,
cold water showers,
my never ending love for them.

Underrating summers,
all my of sweet childhood memories,
my never ending love for them.

If someone asks me about my favourite season,
without a second thought,

I would say summer.

Arun Kashyap

Arun Kashyap belongs to New Delhi, is an English literature student and youth leader of NSS Satyawati College(Eve) D.U.

Dedicated to Social Work and passionately inking his feelings for last three years. His nature and values based writing began from Quotes and now his poems are part of Anthologies 'Ek Goonj', ' Lessons to remember', and ' Whimsy of Creation' and he is Author of ' The Essence of Feelings.'

A LOTS OF GOOD WISHES FOR WONDERFUL JOURNEY AHEAD

Instagram Handle @ arun_kashyap12official

दिल की गर्माहट - गर्मी

विभिन्न प्रकार की ऋतुएं यानी जीवन जीने के विभिन्न रंग और हम भारतवासी अक्सर इस बात पर गर्व भी करते हैं कि भारत विविधताओं का देश है और इन विविधताओं को हम भली भांति जीते हैं, और भारतीय होने पर गर्व भी महसूस करते हैं। कभी-कभी आपको नहीं लगता कि हर एक ऋतु का अपना अलग मजा है? गर्मी,सर्दी, बरसात या फिर वसंत सभी का अपना महत्व है, सभी अपनी जगह खूबसूरत हैं बिल्कुल रंगों की तरह पर आपको किसमें सबसे ज्यादा ख़ुशी मिलती है और किसके साथ आप अधिक जुड़ा हुआ महसूस करते हैं, इन्हीं सब वजहों से कोई भी चीज आपके लिए बेहद ख़ास बन जाती है।

उत्तर भारत का शहर और देश की राजधानी दिल्ली में गर्मी अप्रैल के मध्य दिनों से होनी शुरू हो जाती है और लगभग मध्य जुलाई तक रहती है, इसके बाद मानसून का आगाज़ हो ही जाता है। होली के बाद अप्रैल महीने का आगमन होता है तो इस समय हम नई क्लास में पहुँच जाते थे यह एक नई शुरूआत सी लगती थी, नई-नई किताबें और नोट्सबुक इन पर रंग-बिरंगे कवर चढ़ाना और नई क्लास के माहौल और सिलेबस में ढलना। और इससे भी ख़ास होता था वो इंतज़ार, की अब छुट्टियां पड़ने वाली हैं और डेढ़ महीने की छुट्टियों में ट्रेन में वैठकर नानी के घर जाने को मिलेगा। और इंतजार हो भी क्यों ना? क्योंकि एक साल में एक ही बार तो ऐसा समय आता था, बचपन में इन दिनों तो मेरे मन मे बस रेल का खूबसूरत सफर और नानी के यहाँ का अनोखा प्यार जो मिलता था, उसके ही विचार चलते थे। मई महीने में करीब मम्मी-पापा के साथ जाना होता था यहाँ, और फिर जून में वापसी। लेकिन गर्मी के दिनों कुछ और भी था जो मुझे तरो-ताज़ा रखता था वो था ' अपने दादा जी के

साथ सुबह-सुबह ' मॉर्निंग वॉक ' पर जाना और फिर वहाँ पर साथ में उगते हुए सूरज को देखना। पूर्व दिशा में लाल और हल्के पीलेपन के साथ उगते सूरज को महसूस करना और इसके अर्थ को समझने की कोशिश करना। उसके बाद स्कूल और वहाँ के लौटने के बाद दोपहर में मम्मी-पापा और दादा जी के साथ कभी तरबूज,खरबूज और आम आदि खाना और शाम में दादा जी के साथ रोज शाम को ' सॉफ्ट ड्रिंक पीने जाना और कभी आइसक्रीम का लुत्फ उठाना तो कभी दही-भल्ले का और उनकी बातों को बड़े चाव से सुनना ' कभी यही सब मेरी दुनिया थी। गर्मी के दिन भी बड़े से होते हैं तो दोपहर में लूडो और कैरम बोर्ड खेलकर टाइम पास करना भी मैं कैसे भूल सकता हूँ? इन गर्मी के दिनों को आज भी ऐसे ही जीने की कोशिश करता हूँ पर कहीं ना कहीं अब यह लगता है जिंदगी तो वैसी रही ही नहीं अब। ' दादा जी और नानी जी ' जो मेरे बहुत गहरे दोस्त थे अब बस उनकी यादें, प्यार और आशीर्वाद ही साथ रह गए हैं। क्योंकि गर्मी के दिनों से मेरा रिश्ता यादों का है तो इसलिए यह मेरे दिल के करीब है। " और कहते हैं ना " जब मौजूदा जिंदगी दिलचस्प ना लगे तो गुज़रे हुए पल से कुछ यादें चुराकर अच्छे पलों को जी लेना चाहिए। "

PART-4

Monsoon / मानसून

Akanksha Sakhuja

Akanksha Sakhuja, from Jamshedpur,is a proud alumni of D.B.M.S School. She has presently completed her Graduation in English Honours with flying colours . Her writing gives a way out to her deep and intense passion for literature. She is looking forward to pursue her masters to enhance her qualification. Akanksha is keen on writing good quotes and short stories .Being a good orator she has been an active participant in literary activities in school and at college like debate and speeches etc. Akanksha has a keen interest in reading and to pen down her own experiences which is her uniqueness. She looks forward to teaching and writing as a career. It is just a beginning a long way to go new challenges to overcome.
Instagram Handle @akanksha_sakhuja

Wet Time Of The Year

Each moment of the year has it's own beauty. Seasons make them more colorful and splendid to look at. Each of it has a lot of impact on the mother earth. But, if I talk about my favorite season it is no doubt the Rainy Season . Rain directly reminds me of pent up emotions which leads to tear roll down the eyes give a way to the sad and happy emotions in the heart same as when clouds are filled with water bursts out in a form of rain . The tunder bolt creates a terrifying effect but in contrast the breeze provides a calmness.

If you have ever got a chance to get wet in the rain, you would have experienced the water droplets touching your body creates amazing effect . Even the dry soil petrichor. I really want to feel them again and again . It makes one feel fresh and elevated from this wordly pleasure enjoying each aspect of the nature It is not only cherished by human beings but also by the mother earth. Even animals are energized. The flower starts swaying, the cold breeze and the water droplets on it gives a beautifying effect to it. It's the most pleasant time of the year leaving some sweet and touching memories behind.

Archana devi

Daughter of kannan and sumithra. 1st started writing for her own passion but when she received good comments from people she started to write quotes from different feelings to match others situation and taste. Her works is also published in autumn gales ,an anthology by alcove publications.
Instagram Handle @Kadcraze

Adorable Monsoon

The curtains of the window,
Twirled in roister.
I turned round my chair
And gazed at the window.
I saw a peacock unfurling
It's feather and dancing in joy.
The cool breeze stucked me up
No words can complement,
The feel and love I have for
The mesmerizing monsoon days.
The fragrance of soil filled the air.
Trees swaying its branches in joy.
I turned on the music, nothing
Can stand against the happiness,
I have for this combo!!!

Dr. Ratna Priyanka Bhallamudi

.3

Born to (late) Bhallamudi Venkat Dina mani and bhallamudi vasanta lakshmi. She is a dentist and she got married to Daliparthi venkata girish Sharma. Writing is her hobby and her stress buster
Instagram Handle @Pinks.007

Monsoon

Looked up at the sky to see
And wonder, if the sun was even here
While the clouds take over
To reign over their season
Of this incredible monsoon

The pitter patter
Carries on with its tune
Throughout the night
While the frogs join
Croaking with delight

When the sun dares a peek
The raindrops form a sheet
Together they split the light
Into a colourful sight
To give us the rainbow we await

All the downpour may seem wet,
a few people may detest
But every season has its best
It's the nature's way to replenish
All the bare necessities
For every being to exist

E. Sindhuvarshini

Sindhuvarshini is a authentic and passionate budding writer from Chennai, pursuing UG in law and now experimenting new forms of writings from herself.
Instagram Handle @Sindhuvarshini_eswaran

The Spasm of Mist.

Lassie laughs with blast ,
Where mom losts in thought,
The cloud is par of fog there,
And here , there jumps the frog,
Latter drips loch from puff,
Where men open the buff,
There bloom the Swans in fluff,
Splash sways to solace,
Thus switch of season menace,
Where twitch of reason race,
And now you come to know Lassie's face!

Isha Saraiya

Isha Saraiya is a grade 12th student and a budding psychologist, she has been a part of several anthologies earlier . Writing makes her heart lighter and she has been writing from the age of 13.

She loves to read and draw along with writing.

Instagram handle @_ scribbled.tales _

Monsoon Rains

It was one of those monsoon days when there was thundering and lightning, she was all scared and didn't know how to get back home. There came a stranger with a pup in one hand and an umbrella in the other. He softly told her, ' hey , listen.. let's walk back home together I just shifted to your neighbourhood recently! '. She couldn't identify who this was but she readily accepted the offer.

Walking by the road, holding hands & jumping in the puddles while the rain drizzles it is just the best feeling one ever gets!

That day she just didn't reach home safely but also found a partner for life!

Nivedhitha Patwari

Heyy all soo let me talk something about her. She is Nivedhitha Patwari a fashion designer from Coimbatore, Tamil Nadu with a postive attitude towards everything in life.. As a child she always admired art, but actually it seams to be very beautiful so here i go.. she likes to write and paint which she feel is something creative. She always want to inspire people through her writings. She wants to reach more and more people to share her writeups. Writing is something which cannot be forced upon you. She will always look forward to motivate others and motivate herself. It actually it feels really great to bring back somebody's lost sprit and motivation and writing makes her feel good.
Instagram Handle @lifeline_writeups

A Flash Of Light

Cloud seems like capturing pictures with flash down at us
Something which feels like thunder and lightening in the sky above us
Different people with different thoughts
Some stalking the darkness and
Some Chilling with a relaxed mind
A few of them restoring their lost soul from overthinking....

The point to is relax your mind from getting stressed
Let things happen their way
Which itself will create a new route for a solution..

Samikhya Swain (Ikhya)

Ikhya hails from silver city Cuttack. Currently, she is a student of class 12. Not only a passionate writer, she is also a painter, YouTuber and photographer. Her keen interest in literature made her a writer thus, she believes that words can create wonders. You can connect with her using her Instagram ID @triggered.ladki or simply drop a mail at samikhya123swain@gmail.com

Rain of tears

I walked silently,
With tears brewing in my eycs,
I was heart broken by someone,
Whom I considered to be wise .

There was havoc inside heart,
With beats screaming like thunder.
I looked up to wonder,
Until the first drop of rain,
Skipped down my eyelashes,
Giving relief to my every pain .

With dark clouds over my head,
I headed ahead,
The sky was screaming with thunder,
I felt like it could feel my pain.

I walked slowly and slowly,
Looking here and there abruptly,
Searching for the right place to hide my tears,
I moved ahead near the bay with eyes full of fears.

And guess what?
Even the heaven started crying,
When it felt how my soul is dying.

It started raining so hard,
Letting my tears to depart .

Shijin Ravi C

He is Shijin Ravi C from Kerala.He is pursuing BSc Hons Agriculture graduate.He is a young poet and co-author of many anthologies today. Some of his anthologies are 'The golden words','The uncertain periods','My success ladder','Safar','Her voice','Positive vibes' etc .His mail ID is shijinravi23@gmail.com Instagram Handle @stolen.pearl .

Sound Of Rain

Look like a day after summer to cool,
With the cold breeze and drops of rain,
Started as low as it could but out of hands.
What a day to enjoy in hours of sleep.

Down can the thunder with a flash to smile,
Took my breath for a moment to hell,
Took the earth under its clutch to spell,
Everything so cool outside it's rings.

Me watching everything from the windows,
Loved by the dances in wind,
My mind remained so chill to till,
After all that hours of wash.

With a paper boat prepared to sail,
I went out peeping my mother's call,
A day indeed to drink a soup,
Before I wished it was Infront of hall.

This was the day we all dreamt,
To hear a song and go to sleep,
With all the breeze without the fan,
Filling my heart's with display apart.

Sujitha Ramalingam

This is sujitha. She is a housewife, at the time of lockdown she found herself with the help of paper and pen.
Instagram Handle @stories_of_facts.

Monsoon Blossom

Hi all, I am a tree. Through this story, I am going to describe how we especially enjoyed the monsoon season. This beautiful season starts with our dancing and the beautiful fragrance of the sand. During the summer season, we suffered a lot, because of sunny. Once monsoon starts, our surroundings are filled with chill chill and cool cool.

Once water touches our leaf, all my dryness changed into blossom one. Once the sky starts showering, the childishness inside ours also starts to shower through the dance. Even the stone hearts to melt like ice in the rain season

All my thirsty is fulfilled by rain and we start to grow like bunches with the help of love from the rain. Yeah, we know that there is a connection between ours and rain. Maybe because of that, we love rain instead of the other season. We are all live with the help of this monsoon. If you (human) plant us (trees) then the showers of rain too more.

As we all know that water is the most important thing to live. It's not only for human beings it also for all the living beings like us too. Once the summer season ends, free shower from god starts because of you plant a tree.

Rain - Free gift from God.

Akanksha Sinha

Akanksha Sinha is student by profession ,writer as passion. Lives in Patna, Bihar.She is daughter of Mr. Mukesh kumar and Mrs. Shikha Sinha. She loves to portrait feelings by her poetry and quotes,she likes travelling and capturing moments. Heart healer by birth. She is co author of 15+ anthology. She loves to feel the nature. She is passionate &ambitious for her work.
Currently, she is been a co-author in several anthologies and compiling her first anthology named "Zindagi-Ek-Ehsaas"...
Instagram Handle @merelabzz

बारिश और तुम

बारिश और तुम दोनों एक जैसे हो
बिना बताये आ जाते हो
दिल में उमंगें ले जाते हो
बारिश की बूँदें की तरह
तेरी यादे में मुझे भिगा जाती है

ये जो भीमि सी खुशबू मिट्टी की
जो आती है बारिश के साथ
कुछ इसी तरह ही आती है
तेरी मुझको याद

बारिश में कागज़ की कस्ती में
जो उफान से आता है
वैसे ही कुछ तेरे यादों का
तुफान से आता है

बारिश के साथ कुछ सुकून सा जो आता है
वैसे ही कुछ तुझे देख के दिल सँभाल सा जाता है
बारिश और तुम दोनों एक जैसे हो
बे वक़्त बे वजह दोनों आ जाते हो

Harsha Sharma

Harsha Sharma, 23 years old from Jamshedpur has deep and intense passion in literature. She enjoys to pen down her musings and sentiments. As she concludes: Be Yourself.
Instagram Handle @ harsha4181

बारिश का मौसम है आया,
सब में एक उमंग है लाया।
चारो ओर हरियाली छाई,
तन मन में खुशियाँ है लाया।
वो बरसात में गीली मिट्टी की खुशबू,
और साथ में गरम चाय की प्याली,
सारे जीव जन्तु खुश हैं क्यूंकि,
दिल में है उमंग है छाया।
किसानों की मेहनत पे रंग लाने,
सावन में बादल है गर्जते।
बच्चे-बच्चे खुश हैं अब तो,
देखो पानी में कैसे कागज़ की कश्ती लहराते।

बरसात महज़ एक मौसम नहीं,
ये है एक खुशियों की सौगात।
दिल खोल कर करते हैं लोग इसकी स्वागत,
क्यूंकि इसमें दिखता है सबको अपना बचपन।
ये बारिश की बून्दें हमें हमेशा सिखाती,
ज़िंदगी बस खुश रहने का नाम है।
कैसे छोटी छोटी बातों पर हम यादें बनाये,
और ताउम्र उसे सँजों कर रखें।

Neha Singhania

Hello, introducing Neha Singhania. She is Pursuing CS and a good dancer and a dance tutor too.Writing is her passion, and she want to be a good known writter. She is a part of many anthologies as a co-author . She always try to write on undefined feelings..
Instagram Handle @ dil-e-ehsasss

खुशियो का मौसम

जिसके आने का रहता है इंतेज़ार
जिसके आने से आ जाती है बहार
जिसके आते ही सब सज जाते है
सब के मन खुशियों से भर जाते है
वही तो है मेरा पसंदीदा मौसम -मानसून

जिसके आने से
पेड़ पौधे सब सजने लगते है
सब तरफ हरियाली बसने लगती है
गगन भी खुल के वर्षा करता है
अपने प्रेम को जी भर के लुटाता है
पशु पक्षी भी खिल उठते है
नदी समुंद्र भी भरने लगते है
मोर भी खुल के नृत्य करता है
पक्षियां भी घूम घूम के गाती है
वही तो है मेरा प्यार मौसम-मानसून

मॉनसून आते ही त्यौहार आ जाते है
जैसे सावन ,राखी और कृष्ण जन्माष्टमी
गणेशजी भी घर घर विराजमान रहते है
नए नए भोग, नाच गा सब खूब रिझाते है
मन बहुत खुश सा रहता है
आखिर जन्मदिन भी इसी समय आता है
घर घर खुशियाँ होती है
हर रोज मिठाई बनती है
सबके दिल को उत्सव से भर देती है
यही तो है मेरा प्यार मौसम -मॉनसून

ले कर चाय और किताब हाथ मे
बैठ जाते है बालकनी में
बारिश की छीटों का आनन्द लेते है
साथ ही प्यारे गीत गुनगुनाते है
कभी कभी बारिश में भीग कर नाचते है
तो कभी कागज़ की नाव बना तैराते है
जिसके आते ही
हमारे मन आनंद से भर जाते है
वही तो है मेरा प्यार मौसम-मॉनसून

महिलाओं के सजने सवेंरे का मौसम है ये
झूला झूलने और घूमने का मौसम है ये
प्रेमियों का तो खाश मौसम है ये
सबके दिल के तार जोड़ता मौसम है ये
राधा कृष्णा के प्रेम का मौसम है ये
सब मे प्रेम फैलाने का मौसम है ये
यही तो है मेरा प्यार मौसम -मानसून।

Padma Srivastava

She is from Varanasi. She is a student of Archaeology with it she is also a good writer. She is pursuing graduation from B. H. U. She writes poem since 8th standard. She is fond of singing and writing and composing poetry from starting. She has been co_author of 4 +anthologies except it
Instagram Handle @ @Perfectsriva_quotes

दिलों की ख्वाहिश : ये अनकही बारिश

कभी लगातार बरसती, कभी थम सी जाती है
ये बारिश मुझे तुम्हारी याद दिलाती है
कभी बिजलियों का कड़कना, कभी पानी का झरना
कभी बादलों का यूं बरसना और
फ़िर बारिश का आ जाना
ये सब दिल में कोई अहसास जगाती है
हां बारिश बेशक बहुत पसन्द है मुझे
क्योंकि ये तुम्हारी याद दिलाती है
इन बूंदों का धरती पर आना कोई इत्तेफ़ाक तो नहीं
कहीं ये बूँदे ये बिजली दे रही मुझे आवाज़ तो नहीं
बरसात है या है पैगाम किसी का,,,,,
कोई कर रहा किसी का आगाज़ तो नहीं
सुना है वो किसी मौसम में सजती नहीं है,, तो कहीं
ये बारिश कर रही उसका साज - श्रृंगार तो नहीं
है लग रही ये एक उलझी पहेली,,,
ये दबा हुआ कोई राज़ तो नहीं
कभी बूँदे आती होठों पे,, कभी गुम हो जाती ओसों में
कहीं ये बादल मुझसे नाराज़ तो नहीं
मौसम है सुहावना,,, आंखें मुस्कुराना भी चाहती हैं
हर गली, हर मुहल्ले में घूमकर
बारिश बन जाना चाहती हैं
रंगीन फुहारें, दिलनशीं ख़्याल ,
सुकून भरी यादें दिल में छाती हैं
कभी मुस्कराहट ख़ुद आ जाती इन लब़ों पर,
कभी टूटी ख्वाहिशें खुद ही जुड़ जाती है ,,,
हर ओर सन्नाटा बिखरा और
उन सन्नाटे में कुछ बूँदों का शोर
क्या ऐसे ही बारिश आती है???

हाँ किसी को अच्छी लगती है ये रिमझिम यादें,
तो किसी की जान ले जाती है ,,
कभी खुद बरसने लगती कभी कुछ दीवारें छोड़
सारी महफ़िल को भींगाती है ,,,
क्या ऐसे ही बारिश आती है ???
किसी की यादों से भरी रात और
फ़िर उसमें इन बूँदों की आवाज़
ज़हन में कोई ख्वाहिश जगा रही है
ये अन्दर होने वाली अलग सी ख़ुशी बता रही
शायद मौसम - ए बारिश आ रही है।।

Sahina Ghugha

Sahina Ghugha is 20 year old b.com student at Saurashtra university Rajkot. She is from Jamnagar city of Gujarat. She is state level winner in poetry competition 2017. She is Co-author of 10+ anthologies. She is an amazing writer and poet and she wants do something for society through her pen.
Instagram Handle @Itz_sahina_write

बरसात

गिर रहे धरती के आंचल में,
झरमर झरमर मोती जैसे।
बूंद बूंद कुछ ऐसे गिर रही,
हो आकाश की रानी रोती जैसे।

काली घटाएं , काले बादल,
कुछ कहे रहे है ज़रा गौर से सुनो।
खुशियों का जो इंद्रधनुष है,
इसमें से अपनी पसंद के रंग चुनो।

ये ठंडी हवाएं, ये बहेता पानी,
और मिट्टी की खुश्बू निराली।
ये बरसात की ऋत है बड़ी प्यारी,
मोर का कलरव, हर तरफ हरियाली।

Sarbani Dey

This is Sarbani Dey from Assam.Studying BSC in Maths.Having great interest towards writing poems and alongside she is a trained singer.Love to spent her time nurturing her hobbies.
Instagram Handle @sarbani_dey_

बारिश के मौसम

बारिश के मौसम जैसे मानो,
सूखे पत्तों को जीने की वजह मिल गई हो।।
थोड़ा सा बारिश का पानी जैसे मानो,
ज़मीन को आसमान से जुड़ने की जग़ह ढूंढ ली हो।।
थोड़ा सा पानी के बूंदे जैसे मानो,
प्यास लोगो के प्यासा मिट गई हो।।
आखिर बारिश मौसम है ई ऐसी
जिसे बिगना नही पसंद
वो भी बारिश में झूम झूम कर नाचते है।।
जिसे बारिश नही पसंद
वो भी धूप में बारिश होने की दुआ करते है।।
इन्ही हर एक वजह से
मुझे पसंद है ये बारिश के मौसम।।

Shivika Sharma

Shivika Sharma is a writer. She is a college student.She live in kawardha Chhattisgarh. She loves to write poems, quotes & shayaris etc.She used yourquote app for presenting her views.
Instagram Handle@shivika1108

मेरे प्रिय सावन

बारिश का मौसम है आया,
और मेरे दिल को है धड़काया।
बूंदों से भरा ये मौसम,
सावन का महीना है आया।।

चली मैं भीगने बाहर,
तन पर बूंदें जब गिरती हैं।
तब मेरे मन में ढेर सारी,
खुशियों की बहार सजती हैं।।

मेरे हृदय पर अनेकों उल्लास का,
घनघोर घटा है छाया।
हाय!रे मेरे सावन,
खुशियों की सौगात है लाया।।

बूंद जब चेहरे पर पड़ती है,
मेरे दिल में हलचल मच जाती हैं।
और ये सावन के महीने में,
ढेर सारी खुशियां आ जाती हैं।।

Urvashi Patel

Urvashi Patel, She is student of Bachelor of computer application..She is from Diamond city Surat,Gujarat..She is not professional writer, but she likes writing about different different topic... She is hard working girl...She called her 'Smilelover' because she's face always smiling...She was worked in 10+ anthologies as a co-author...
Instagram Handle
@world_of_feeling_in_word & @smilelover_06

बारिश

मुझे बारिश बहुत पसंद है।
वो आसमान में धीरे धीरे उमड़ते पानी से भरे हुए बादल जैसे दिल में उमड़ती हुई प्यारी सी यादे।
बादलों के पीछे वो छुपा हुआ सूरज जैसे खुशियों के पीछे छुपा हुआ गम ।
ठंडी सी लहराती पवन जैसे किसी खास इंसान कि यादे।
वो मोर का अपने नाच के साथ बरसात को बुलाना और मेंढक की टर टर जैसे कोई अपने खास को बुला रहा हो।
और फिर धीरे धीरे बारिश आना और तन को भिगोना जैसे किसी खास का अहसास होना।
बारिश की बूंदों का यूं तन को भिगोना और
किसी खास की यादों में मन का भीग जाना।
वह बारिश में पी हुई गर्म चाय जैसे वो खास का अपने साथ होना।
और गर्म गर्म पकोड़े जैसे किसी खास का प्यार मिल जाना।

PART-5

Fall/Autumn

/ पतझड़

Aditi Debnath

This is Aditi Debnath. She is a student, poetess, writer, and an artist. She is from MP, born and raised in Jabalpur and she is pursuing BA. She is a kind of girl who feed on poetries, paint with words and wears words on her sleeves. She has a magical skill to turn any blank page into teeming concerts of words. Food is what her soul is made for. She is one of those person who takes the long way home just to listen to more songs and still probably she might be vibing into her current favorite song. She also portrays and sketches her imaginations and events of her life into her canvas. She solemnly believes on the fact that you only live once and by this she is trying to live her life to the fullest.
Instagram Handle @aditively

The Aroma Of Autumn

The nerveless chilly bite in the dawn air.
Everyone is getting excited for the harvest fair.
The slowly coming of sun to shine over the blue skies.
Kids are eagerly waiting, to eat different kind of pies.
The smell of nutmeg and cloves, coming from around every corner.
Wearing of scarfs, socks and oversized sweaters to keep us warmer.
Collecting pretty leaves, to rake up and jump into them later.
Going on a hayride, our feelings get greater.
Frost get collected, on each blade of grass.
Decorating the interior with pine cones, leaves, and small squash.
Tying up the jacket around the waist, as the day heats up from the cold morning.
Buying fall-scented candles for the night adorning.
Going for hikes in the forest, as mushroom picking trips.
Drinking cinnamon-spiced tea, relishing it sip by sip.
Making of finger licking caramel-dipped apples.
Going for prayer, and singing hymns at chapels.
The crunching of leaves, beneath our shoes.
Bare branches looks scarier against the harvest moon.
Walking by a place that is said to be haunted.
Carving funny faces in pumpkins, as everyone wanted.
Grumbling of stomach, by the smell of buttery yams.
And a big fat family dinner involving turkey or ham.
Taking selfies, and posing weirdly for family photos.
Getting over excited for fall seasonal sports.
Celebrating and enjoying beside the warm bonfire.
Singing and dancing; flaunting the fall attire.
Getting lost in admiring the different hues of the fallen leaves.
People welcoming the autumn, by decorating the door with autumn wreaths.

The red beauty of nature has now come to life.
The season of falling leaves finally has arrived.
This is the year's last loveliest smile, that cannot be compare.
The aroma of autumn season, spreading joy and zeal everywhere.

Jude Fernandes

Currently pursuing a Masters in English from Goa University - Taleigao, Jude is an enthusiastic student residing in Vasco da Gama, Goa - India.
Instagram Handle @jude_fernandes_official

The Falling Leaves...

Gorgeous October, I adore you!
Preceding the shivers
of chill and freeze...
Autumn is welcomed
with the shedding of leaves!

Timber arms, increasingly bare!
Lush shades of orange
turn pale and dry...
Winds blow flying kisses
as leaves fall to the ground!

Watch the landscape transform!
Wilted leaves crunch
under hooves and footsteps...
Dryness isn't deficiency;
nature paves way for new life!

Prittam Bhattacharyya

Prittam Bhattacharyya is from Kolkata, the city of joy. Currently pursuing a Bachelor's of Computer Applications. Writing is his passion, his way of expressing his innermost emotions. Every now and then he writes stories, poems, and lyrics of songs. He always likes to be a part of any artistic community. To him, art is something which brings people together. He wishes to write many stories and poems in the coming days. He has interest in stuff related to computers and electronics, such as programming, game and graphics designing, and robotics. He has also been a part of over 50 anthologies.

Instagram Handle @Prittam3000

Gentle Autumn

Still, there's another autumn
That cools you when it's warm
But isn't too cold to chill
A season that brushes against your cheeks
Even so gently and sweetly

Walk calmly during the fall
Let it fade your worries away
As does the green in the leaves
Just like the yellow and red tinted foliage
Be warm and bright inside

Night comes earlier
To rest you more at night
This is autumn
The season for harvesting
Harvest your food for your body

And your spirit for your life
Harvest the good cheer
And loving fruit in your heart
So that you can share with others
During the holidays to come

And so that is autumn
And as the leaves fall
And with the degrees drop
Cause the friendly affectionate season
Will end and winter will begin

Rashi Sunder

A student . Currently pursuing Law . loves to paint, write and help.
Instagram Handle @ rashi_sunder

The Season of Maturity

When Lcaves turn red and yellow,
And lays on the ground,
Then it's the time, my dear fellow,
You will walk and hear that rustling sound.
The immense beautification of the nature,
When it sheds all what is unwanted,
Giving us the signal to be mature,
And to get rid of all those who always taunted .
In the midst of dropping temperature,
It is the time to seek comfort,
Stay healthy and enjoy the nature,
But do not forget to the dirt.
Yes, it is autumn, it is fall,
Move out and be a gall.

Time for Rejuvenation

It's cloudy, rainy and wet,
The nature is trying to rejuvenate,
You know it, I bet,
Yes, this season is my favorite.
The hustling and rustling of the leaves,
Long coats, warm shades,
It's time for full sleeves,
Can you guess this charade?
Let me tell you people,
It is autumn, the season of prosperity,
Bring out the bottle of your maple,
And be ready in solidarity.

Soma Das

Soma Das is from Jamshedpur who is a proud alumunai of Kerala Public School. She has completed her graduation in English honors. She has developed a keen interest in writing after she started nurturing over the novels. She is a very good learner and always awaits for new topics and lessons to learn. Her decided profession is to become a teacher as well as a writer for which she is preparing herself at the fullest.
Instagram Handle @soma_das

The Autumn Season

When the leaves of the trees starts turning from green to red , yellow and orange,
When the days start becoming shorter and the night becomes longer,
I understand this is the season I await for the whole year,
That is my lovely season, The Autumn Season.
The season which brings alot of fun,
The season that gives a delight to everyone,
The season which energize everyone,
And ask to get ready for outdoor fun.
The season which provides rest to all the creatures,
The season which allow us for some adventures,
The season that I await for the whole year,
That is my lovely season, The Autumn Season.
Though in this season the trees shed their leaves,
But still the nature looks pleasing.
Though in this season the weather is a bit cold,
But keeps everyone's mind consoled .
Though in this season there are alot of pros and cons,
But mine favourite season would always be the same,
That is my lovely season, The Autumn Season.

Ujjwal Shree

Ujjwal shree with her pen name Neha Gupta is from Patna, Bihar She is an avid writer, poetess, and artist. She loves to play with words and write from the depth of her heart. She always express her emotions through words rather than saying. She generalltes about Motivation, emotions, pain and abstract. Writing helps her to survive in her worst phase of life. Writing is just like breathing to her because when she feels depressed she used to write her feelings.

Instagram Handle @Shree22349
Email Id : ng223494@gmail.com

The Season of Fall

The soft serenade of autumn after the high notes of endlessly humid summer is refreshing, uplifting and yet cozy. My favorite thing about fall is

•Windy weather freshens you up

Nothing beats getting you into a better mood than windy weather. When you go outside when it's windy, the wind might destroy a carefully styled hairdo, but, more importantly, will definitely blow away your worries, sorrows, bad moods and the like.

•Autumn equals fabulous food

Autumn is a season that offers so much joy . How about different wild game dishes with cabbage, mushrooms and other veggies?

•Soft fabrics hug you

Autumn is also the season in which you transfer your warmer and softer clothes to that part of your wardrobe where you can easily grab them.

•A walk in the forest stimulates your senses

When you are not the "windy walk" type, you may want to go for a walk in a park or forest among colourful leaves.You will enjoy what you see, what you hear, what you feel and what you smell on an autumn walk in a park or forest. It's an excellent training for your senses and the more you are aware of your senses, the more you pick up from your surroundings. A walk in the woods may be relaxing and stimulating at the same time. You will come home full of energy!

The whole energy of autumn is a time for serious renewal in my life, and has always been so! I just delight in Fall. I always feel pretty ambitious.

www.ingramcontent.com/pod-product-compliance
Ingram Content Group UK Ltd.
Pitfield, Milton Keynes, MK11 3LW, UK
UKHW022005190726
13853UKWH00004B/1750